In outer space
It's black as night
And something's moving—
Speed of light—
Something looking
for a fight...

THE ALIENS ARE COMING!

Colin McNaughton

CANDLEWICK PRESS
CAMBRIDGE, MASSACHUSETTS

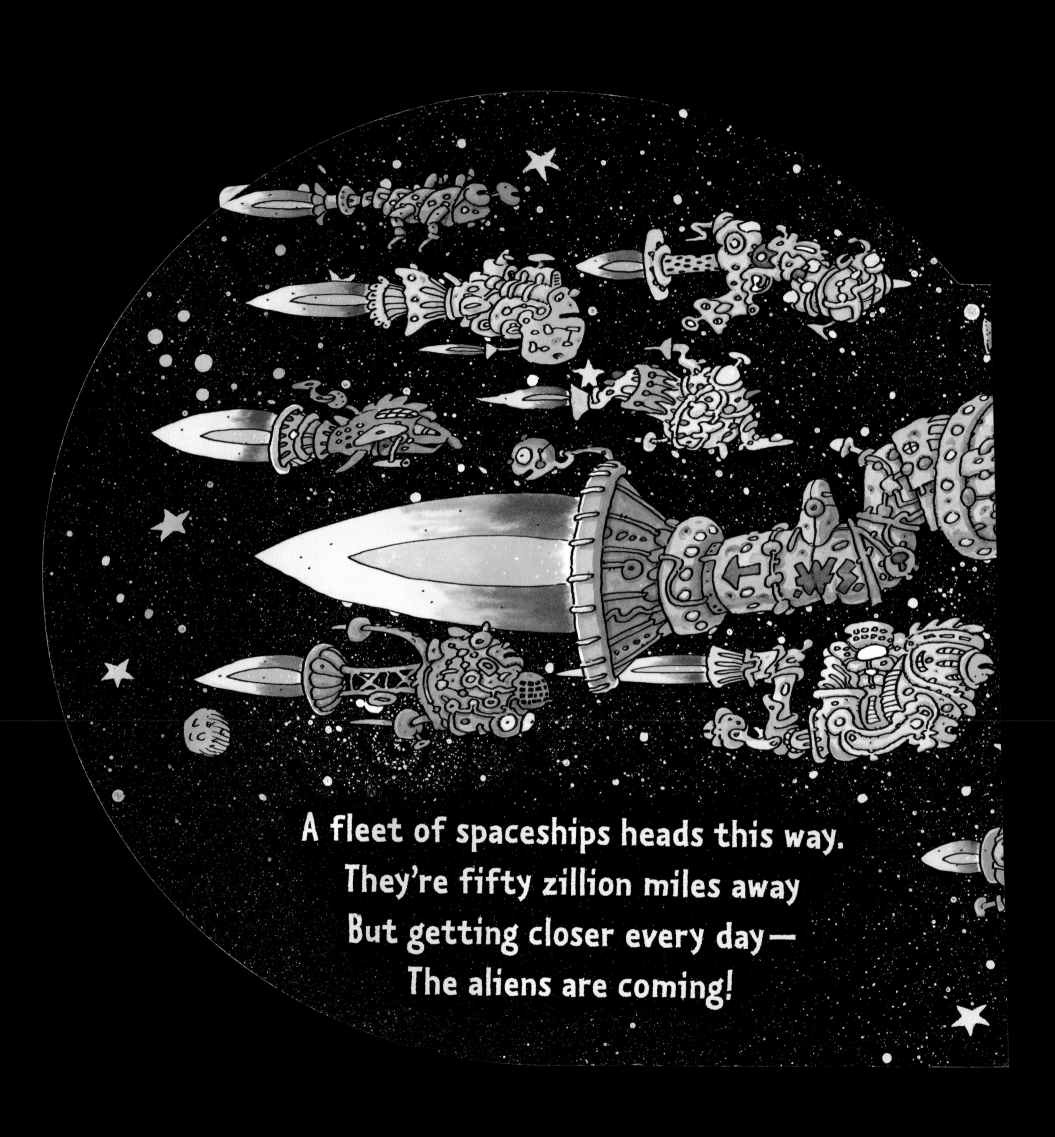

A fleet of spaceships heads this way.
They're fifty zillion miles away
But getting closer every day—
The aliens are coming!

They're zooming in from outer space
To conquer us, the human race.
We'll soon be standing face to face—
The aliens are coming!

The admiral's a fearsome sight—
A simple creature, not too bright;
All he wants to do is FIGHT!
The aliens are coming!

The first mate looks like wobbly jelly,
He's sort of gaseous and he's smelly;
He has an eyeball on his belly!
The aliens are coming!

These beings come in different sizes—
This one's doing exercises.
Get ready, Earth, for some surprises—
The aliens are coming!

Some have one head—some have two.
(There's even one with none, it's true!)
What on earth are we to do?
The aliens are coming!

They come from planets near and far—
Some big, some small, some quite bizarre.

Twinkle, twinkle, little star—
The aliens are coming!

I really hate to make a fuss
(Perhaps you thought they'd look like us),
But most of them appear thus.
The aliens are coming!

This one squeaks and that one squawks;
Some have eyeballs stuck on stalks.
This one squelches when it walks.
The aliens are coming!

See the aliens at lunch:
Slobber, dribble, gobble, munch.
Table manners? Not this bunch.
The aliens are coming!

Some are bald and some are hairy,
Some are roundy—some are squary.
Some look friendly but beware—
The aliens are coming!

They've boldly been where we've not been;
They're blue and purple, sickly green.
(At home this one's a beauty queen!)
The aliens are coming!

None speak English, French, or Greek.
They sort of grunt and burp and squeak.

The chance of peace talks? I'd say BLEAK!
The aliens are coming!

This one biffs and that one bops,
This one nips and that one chops.
Someone better call the cops!
The aliens are coming!

Some are tall and some are squat,
Some are cool and some are hot.
Some are nice but most are not!
The aliens are coming!

At last the earth comes into view.
The admiral knows what to do.
He orders, "BATTLE STATIONS, CREW!"
The aliens are coming!
BUT!
Looking through his telescope,
Suddenly he lost all hope;
He knew his army couldn't cope.
The aliens are slowing!

The admiral jumped up and cried,
"CHANGE OF ORDERS—RUN AND HIDE!"
The aliens were TERRIFIED!
The aliens are going!

For this is what the aliens saw:
PEEKABOO—IT'S **YOU**! What's more,
You've scared them off—away they roar.
The aliens are going!

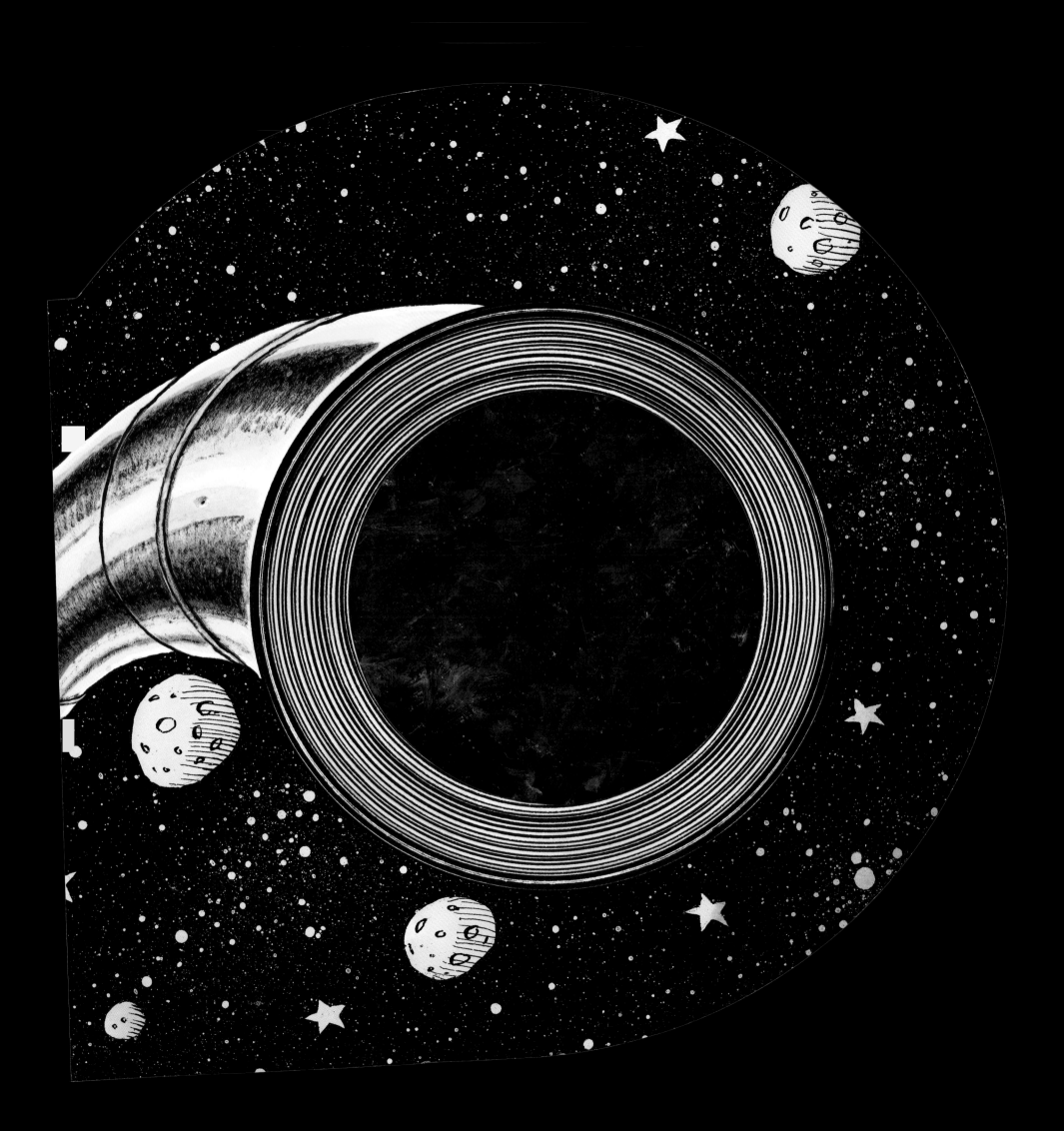

Of life in every galaxy,
The scariest is you—YIPPEE!
You've saved the world, just look and see.
The aliens are gone, HOORAY!
The aliens are gone!